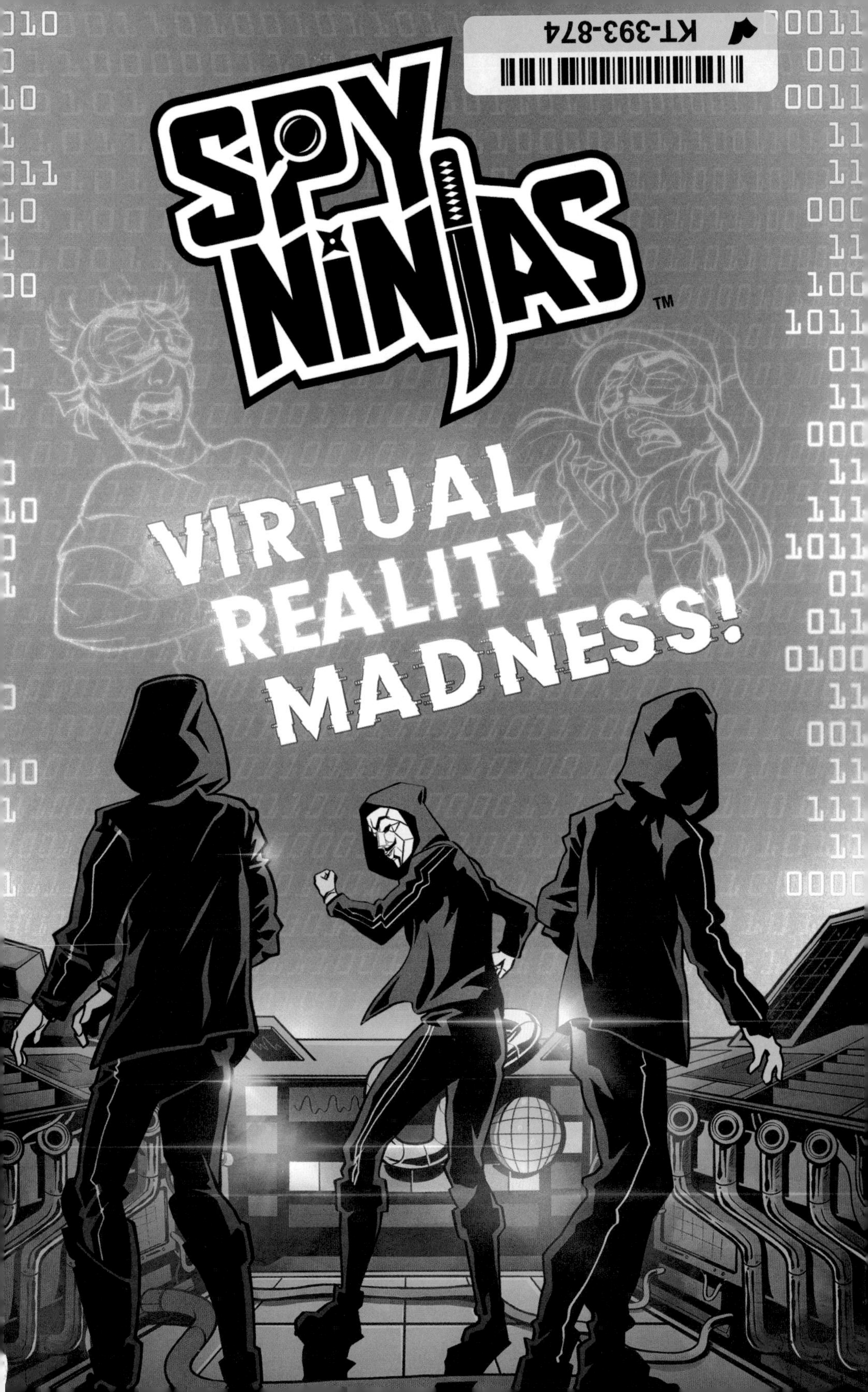
SPY NINJAS™
VIRTUAL
REALITY
MADNESS!

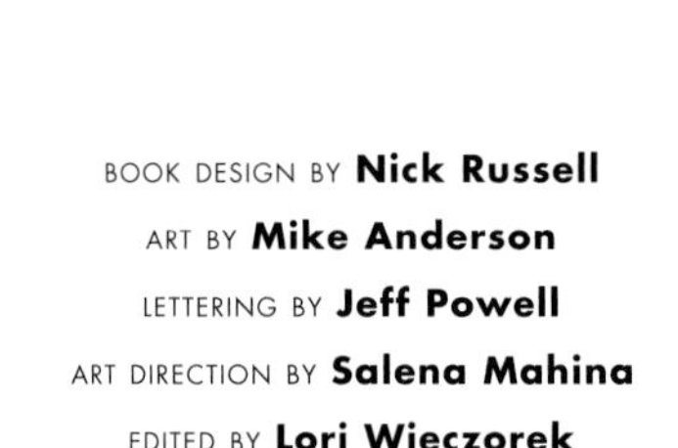

BOOK DESIGN BY **Nick Russell**

ART BY **Mike Anderson**

LETTERING BY **Jeff Powell**

ART DIRECTION BY **Salena Mahina**

EDITED BY **Lori Wieczorek**

ISBN 978-1-338-81461-3

10 9 8 7 6 5 4 3 2 22 23 24 25 26

Printed in the U.S.A. 40

First printing 2022

VIRTUAL REALITY MADNESS!

WRITTEN BY
VANNOTES
ILLUSTRATED BY
MIKE ANDERSON

CHAPTER 1

THEY ARE THE SPY NINJAS, a team of YouTubers on a mission to save the internet from Project Zorgo, an evil organization of hackers. By combining martial arts, stealth, detective work, and hacking, the team works to uncover Project Zorgo's nefarious plans and stop them from taking over YouTube, Roblox, and the rest of the internet.
PZ9 COMPUTER COMPANY
HACKERS RULE
CADEN
WAZ HERE
I'M OUT OF SPRAYPAINT
HAIL the TYPEWRITER
PZ9 lives

SPY NINJA OPERATION
CODENAME: Cheat Coders
OBJECTIVE: To collect old Project Zorgo technology to prevent future hacking
STATUS: In progress
WAS THIS REALLY PROJECT ZORGO'S OLD SECRET LAB?
THIS IS WHERE THEY LAUNCHED SOME OF THEIR CYBERATTACKS ON THE SPY NINJAS! BEEN A LONG TIME SINCE I'VE SEEN THIS PLACE. IT LOOKED A LOT BETTER THEN.

SPY NINJA NAME: Chad Wild Clay
SKILLS: Ninja weapons expert
FUN FACT: Has over 10,000 Spider-Man comic books.
LET'S SEE IF THERE ARE ANY CLUES THAT WILL STOP THEIR EVIL HACKING ONCE AND FOR ALL.
SPY NINJA NAME: Vy Qwaint
SKILLS: Lock picking & fitting through tight spaces
FUN FACT: Will eat pho soup even on a hot summer day.
WHY DO I FEEL LIKE WE'RE BEING WATCHED?
MY SPY JAMMER IS ON! IF THERE ARE ANY LEFTOVER SECURITY CAMERAS, THEY WON'T DETECT US.
SPY NINJA NAME: Daniel Gizmo
SKILLS: Collecting old & new Spy Gadgets
FAVORITE THING: Foot-long subs
SPY NINJA NAME: Melvin PZ9
SKILLS: Gamer & fighter
FAVORITE THING: Hitting the gym
AND IF ANY LEFTOVER HACKERS ARE CRAWLING AROUND, I CAN TAKE THEM OUT.
I DOUBT ANYONE HAS STUCK AROUND THIS PLACE. WAS THAT A TWO-HEADED RAT?
SPY NINJA NAME: Regina Ginera
SKILLS: Master of disguise
FAVORITE THING: Chicken nuggets

I'M SURE THERE ARE ALL SORTS OF DIABOLICAL SUPERVILLAIN WEAPONS IN HERE!
OKAY, MAYBE THAT ONE'S NOT TOO GREAT . . .
DOOMICYCLE
OR THAT ONE . . .
RAIN OF PUNCHES
MAN, THEY WEREN'T EVEN TRYING WITH THIS ONE.
PLUNGECHUCK
THIS MISSION IS A BUST.
WAIT, WHAT'S THAT?

WHOA! WHAT ARE THESE?
THEY LOOK LIKE VIRTUAL REALITY HEADSETS.
I HEARD PROJECT ZORGO MIGHT HAVE BEEN WORKING ON ADVANCED VR TECHNOLOGY.
THEY MIGHT BE PROTOTYPES FOR THE MIND CONTROL DEVICES THEY'VE USED ON US BEFORE.

AT LEAST WE'RE WALKING OUT OF HERE WITH SOME-THING.
Y'KNOW . . . MAYBE IF I TAKE THIS APART IT'LL BE MORE USEFUL.
SPY NINJAS SAFE HOUSE
Y'KNOW, EVEN THOUGH MOST OF THOSE ANTI-SPY NINJA INVENTIONS WERE LAME . . .
THESE SEEM TO BE TRAINING SIMULATORS FOR PROJECT ZORGO HACKERS SO THEY CAN LEVEL UP SUPERFAST.

WAIT, SO THEY'RE LIKE SUPERVILLAIN GAMES?
OH NO! ANOTHER VIDEO GAME FOR YOU TO BEAT ME AT!
VY, IF YOU CAN PLAY WITH ME, I'LL CLEAN ALL OUR TOILETS FOR A MONTH.
OH, ALRIGHT.
NO WAIT! CHAD! VY! WE DON'T KNOW IF—
THEY'RE A TRAP!
MAYBE VIDEO GAMES DO TURN YOUR BRAIN INTO MASHED POTATOES!
TOO SOON, BRO.

UGH... THEY'RE LOCKED ON TIGHT.
CAN YOU HEAR ME, VY?
YEAH, THEY'RE OUT OF IT.
I DIDN'T GET TO RUN ENOUGH TESTS. WHO KNOWS WHAT THESE HEADSETS ARE ACTUALLY CAPABLE OF.
I GUESS WE CAN'T JUST LEAVE THEM ON THE GROUND LIKE THIS.

"I WONDER WHAT THEY'RE SEEING?"
CHAD...
I DON'T THINK WE'RE IN LAS VEGAS ANYMORE.

WELCOME, PLAYERS!
G'DAY, MATES! I'M SLY MARSUPIAL AND I'M YOUR OFFICIAL GUIDE TO SUPER ZORGOLAND: THE VIDEO GAME!
WE HAVE TO GET AWAY FROM THAT THING AS FAST AS POSSIBLE.
I DON'T KNOW. I THINK IT'S KIND OF CUTE.
NOT SO FAST, PLAYER 2! YOU WON'T BE GETTING AWAY FROM ME ANYTIME SOON.
BECAUSE YOU CAN NEVER LEAVE SUPER ZORGOLAND.

WAIT! WHAT DO YOU MEAN?
WHY WOULD YOU EVER WANT TO LEAVE THIS AMAZING VIDEO GAME THAT PROJECT ZORGO HAS CREATED FOR ITS PLAYERS?
I GUESS IF YOU BEAT THE FINAL BOSS, THERE'S A SAVE POINT FOR A BATHROOM BREAK . . . BUT . . .
PERFECT! THERE'S NEVER BEEN A VIDEO GAME THAT THE SPY NINJAS CAN'T BEAT.
OF COURSE, IF YOU LOSE ALL THREE OF YOUR LIVES BEFORE THE END, THE HEADSETS WILL WIPE YOUR MINDS SO YOU CAN ENJOY THE VIDEO GAME ALL OVER AGAIN . . . AND AGAIN . . . AND AGAIN.
AND YOU'LL LOSE EVERY SINGLE MEMORY OF YOUR FRIENDS AND FAMILY, REPLACED WITH EVEN BETTER PROGRAMMING!

WHAT DO YOU THINK OF THIS MUSTACHE?
YOUR FINEST WORK YET.

OKAY, SO I EXAMINED THE SCHEMATICS OF THESE DEVICES AND . . .

OH COME ON, GUYS!

YOU TOOK ALL THE GOOD REAL ESTATE . . .

SPY NINJAS!

WE KNOW YOU TOOK OUR VR HEADSETS!
FINDERS KEEPERS, HACKERS.
WHAT HAVE YOU DONE WITH CHAD AND VY?
HAHA! THE SPY NINJA'S TWO LEADERS WERE FOOLISH ENOUGH TO PUT ON OUR BOOBY-TRAPPED HEADSETS.
WE THOUGHT YOU'D SIMPLY FALLEN FOR OUR SECRET TRACKING DEVICE SCHEME. THEN THIS TRULY IS THE PERFECT TIME TO STRIKE!

PREPARE YOURSELVES, SPY NINJAS! WE HAVE TRIANGULATED THE LOCATION OF YOUR SAFE HOUSE.
DON'T THEY KNOW WHERE WE LIVE YET?
YEAH, HOW MANY TIMES HAVE THEY ATTACKED OUR SAFE HOUSE?
LISTEN, WE JUST KEEP FORGETTING TO SAVE YOUR ADDRESS IN OUR PHONES...
THIS TIME THOUGH, WE'RE NOT GOING TO LEAVE IT IN ONE PIECE!
ALRIGHT, TEAM. GET READY. IT'S GOING TO BE THREE AGAINST... WHO KNOWS HOW MANY...

THIS IS THE END OF THE SPY NINJAS. ASSEMBLE OUR BEST HACKERS, AND JUST IN CASE. . . PREPARE PROJECT ZORGOMONGOUS!

CHAPTER 2

AAAAAHHHHH!
GET READY, PLAYER 1 AND PLAYER 2! THE TUTORIAL IS OVER. YOU ARE NOW READY FOR LEVEL 1!
YOU MIGHT EXPERIENCE SOME DISCOMFORT AS YOUR DIGITAL CODE IS REASSEMBLED TO BETTER SUIT THE EXPERIENCE.
OOOF!

WHOA!
ULTIMATE OBBY TOWER
THAT TOWER LOOKS LIKE WHAT I ALWAYS WANTED FOR MY BIRTHDAY.

ULTIMATE OBBY TOWER
ALRIGHT, SLY, HOW DO WE BEAT THE LEVEL?
YOU'LL NEED TO GET TO THE TOP. THIS WILL TEST NOT ONLY YOUR ABILITY TO CLIMB THE TOWER, BUT YOUR WITS AS WELL.
NO SWEAT! WE DO OBSTACLE COURSES IN TRAINING ALL THE TIME.
YOU'RE RIGHT! HOW HARD CAN THIS ONE BE?

I'D ASK THEM. THEY WERE PLAYERS WHO LOST ALL THEIR LIVES ON THIS LEVEL ALONE.

PROJECT ZORGO'S ALREADY ENSNARED ALL OF THEM?
YES, AND WITH OUR PLAN TO ADD PZ CHIPS INTO EVERY VR HEADSET IN THE WORLD . . .
SOON YOU'LL HAVE EVEN MORE PLAYERS TO INTERACT WITH.
WE HAVE TO WIN THIS GAME, VY. FOR ALL THESE POOR PEOPLE.
WE CAN'T LOSE OUR COOL, THOUGH. WE'LL JUST TREAT IT LIKE WE WOULD ANY OTHER VIDEO GAME.
I GUESS . . .

LAST TO THE TOP HAS TO SMELL MELVIN'S DIRTY SOCKS.
PLAYER 2 HAS IT RIGHT! THE BEST WAY TO PLAY IS TO RUSH AHEAD!
Y'KNOW, THIS ISN'T BAD FOR SOMEONE WITH SPY NINJA TRAINING.
BUT IT'LL BE HARD CATCHING UP TO VY. SHE'S SO GOOD AT ZIPPING THROUGH ALL THESE FLOATING OBSTACLES.

WAIT! IS THAT LAVA?
OOOF!

WELL, THIS ISN'T GOOD.
CHAD!

THAT DIDN'T FAKE-HURT . . . THAT *ACTUALLY* HURT!
I'M SURE THAT WAS A GOOD LEARNING EXPERIENCE FOR YOU, PLAYER 1.
C'MON, SLOWPOKE. IT'S ALWAYS EASY TO LOSE YOUR FIRST LIFE.

THERE MAY BE A LOT GOING ON AND YOU MIGHT BE MORE AWKWARD AT NAVIGATING TIGHT SPACES THAN VY, BUT REMEMBER YOUR TRAINING.

STILL GOT IT.

OKAY, NOW FORGET YOUR COOL NINJA TRAINING AND REMEMBER EVERY MOVIE YOU'VE EVER WATCHED, CHAD.

LOOKING COOL IS DEFINITELY *NOT* A PRIORITY WHEN CROSSING ROPE BRIDGES.

WHAT WAS THE EARLIEST VIDEO GAME?

SPACEWARS!

PONG

SPACE INVADERS

FIGURED I'D WAIT FOR YOU FOR THE TRIVIA . . . JUST IN CASE YOU DIDN'T KNOW IT.

I'M SURE YOU GET THE GIST OF THIS OBSTACLE, BUT THOUGHT I'D LET YOU KNOW . . .
PONG
WE HAVE TO CHOOSE THE RIGHT DOOR OR WE'LL LOSE A LIFE.
I'VE GOT THIS!
ARE YOU SURE? YOU'VE ALREADY LOST ONE LIFE.
IT'S LIKE ANY CLASSIC OBBY. NONE OF THEM ARE CORRECT.
SPACE INVADERS
HMM . . .

THERE! I THINK WE HAVE TO ENTER FROM THIS SIDE. A LOT OF PEOPLE REMEMBER *PONG*, BUT IN 1958 WILLIAM HIGINBOTHAM PROGRAMMED THE ORIGINAL *TENNIS FOR TWO!*
TENNIS FOR TWO
WHICH IS A SIMILAR GAME FROM ANOTHER PERSPECTIVE.

TRUST ME?
100%!

NIS FOR TWO

WE'RE ALIVE! OH MY GOSH, I WAS SO WORRIED.
I THOUGHT YOU SAID YOU TRUSTED ME?!

I DO!
WELL, WE'RE IN THE CLEAR NOW. THAT'S THE TOP OF THE TOWER!

GROOOOOAAAAAAAANN

YOU JUST ***HAD*** TO JINX US.

HOW'S IT GOING, *TOWER BOSS?* BEEN A WHILE SINCE WE'VE HAD TWO PLAYERS WHO'VE MADE IT THIS FAR.
I DIDN'T KNOW A VIDEO GAME COULD BE SUCH A WORKOUT!
JUMP BACK, VY!

WHUM
IF THERE'S ANYTHING I'VE LEARNED ON THIS LEVEL, IT'S THAT SOMETIMES YOU HAVE TO TAKE A STEP BACKWARD . . .

TO MOVE FORWARD.

WAHHOOOO!
ON TO LEVEL 2!

MELVIN, HAVE YOU SEEN MY DISGUISE KIT?
NO! HAVE YOU SEEN THAT PLUNGE-CHUCK?
EWWW! NO!
OH, THERE IT IS!
NOW IF ONLY I COULD FIND MY PLUNGECHUCK . . .
DON'T WORRY, YOU TWO. WE'LL GET YOU OUT OF THERE.
BUT FIRST WE HAVE TO HIDE YOU IN A SAFE PLACE WHILE PROJECT ZORGO LAUNCHES THEIR ATTACK ON OUR HOUSE.

DID PROJECT ZORGO CHICKEN OUT? WHERE ARE THEY?
THEY ARE NORMALLY ON OUR FRONT DOOR ONCE THEY'VE MADE A BORING SPEECH ABOUT HOW THEY'LL DESTROY THE SPY NINJAS.
BUT THEY'RE NOWHERE TO BE SEEN.

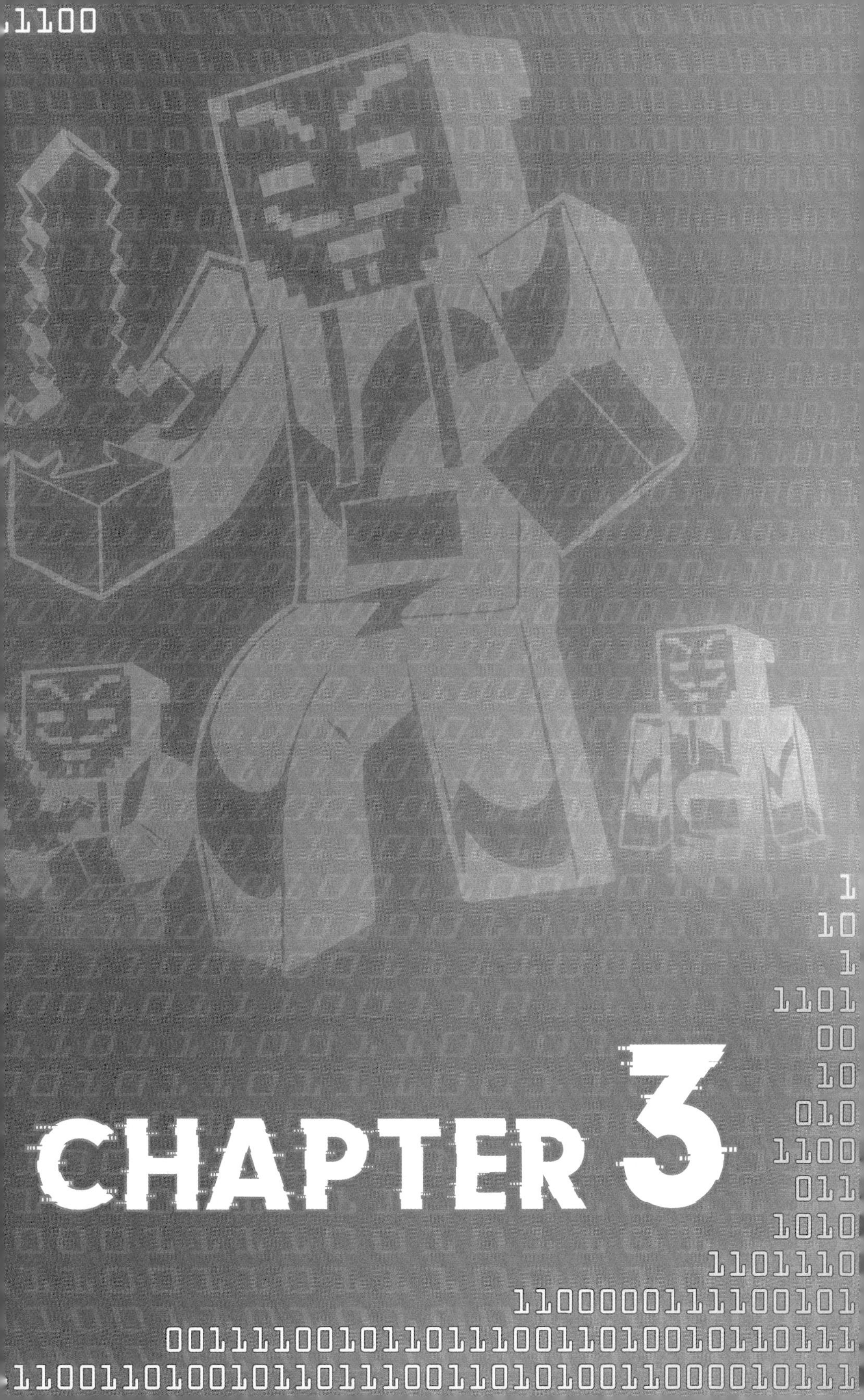

CHAPTER 3

THUMP THUMP
THUMP THUMP
SOMETHING TELLS ME THEY'RE NOT COMING THROUGH THE FRONT DOOR.

Craft Quest
NOW THAT YOU'VE LEARNED THE ROPES (AND THE BLOCKS), WHY NOT PUT YOUR SKILLS TO THE TEST! YOU'LL NEED TO GRAB THE PROJECT ZORGO CUBE AT THE TOP OF THAT TEMPLE TO LEAVE.

WHOA! DID I LOSE SOME POLYGONS?
YOU REALLY ARE A BLOCKHEAD NOW!

PLAYERS! YOU'RE THE FIRST IN MANY HEROIC AGES TO MAKE IT TO MY LEVEL!

UGH! I CAN'T STAND THIS GUY!
HE'S WAY TOO TALKATIVE. TOTAL MANSPLAINER.

CLANG
OOOF!
CRASH
BONK

LATER!
ARE YOU OKAY, SIR?
WAIT, VY!

ANYONE COULD BE AN ENEMY IN THIS GAME...

OH, DON'T WORRY— I'M NOT AN ENEMY.

THOSE ARE YOUR ENEMIES.

I'M JUST HERE TO HELP YOU LEARN THE ART OF CRAFTING.

OH, GREAT . . .

NO, NO, NO. THE MAGIC OF *CRAFT QUEST* IS MAKING YOUR OWN WEAPONS, LIKE PROJECT ZORGO HACKERS OFTEN HAVE TO DO IN THE FIELD.

LET ME SHOW YOU.

COMBINE!
WAIT. . .HOW DOES A PIG AND A . . .?

Oink!

NOPE, NOPE, NOPE, NOPE, NOPE!

I THINK WE'LL BE FINE WITH JUST SOME REGULAR GEAR.
SEE YOU, OLD MAN!

BUT WAIT! WHAT ABOUT THE WONDERS OF CRAFTING?
I'VE GOT AN IDEA, VY. I'M NOT RISKING ANOTHER LIFE FIGHTING MONSTERS AGAIN.

NO WAY I'M GOING THROUGH AN ENTIRE TEMPLE FULL OF TRAPS AND ENEMIES WITH ONLY TWO LIVES.
CRAFTING'S MORE FUN WITH GLITTER, ANYWAY . . .

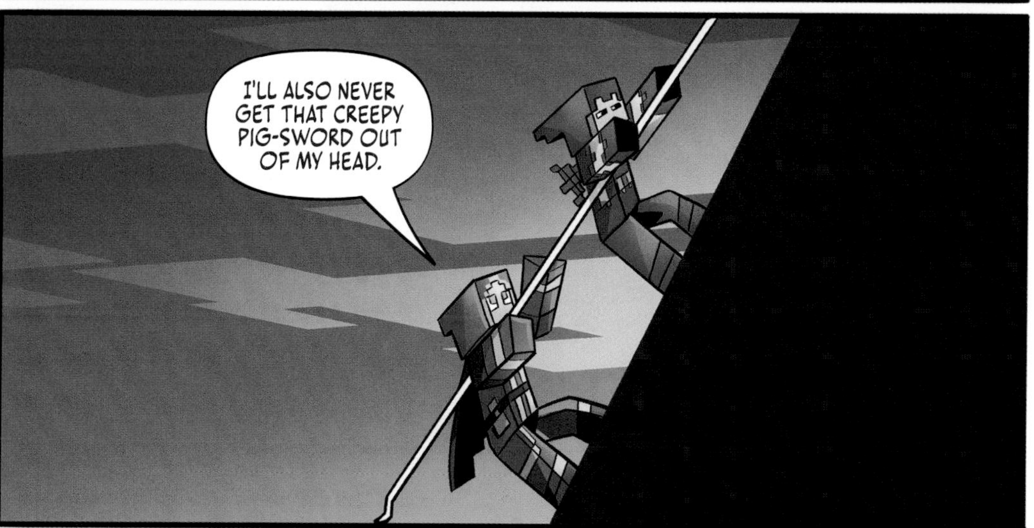
I'LL ALSO NEVER GET THAT CREEPY PIG-SWORD OUT OF MY HEAD.

YOU BROKE THE RULES, PLAYERS.

THE POINT OF THE GAME IS TO COLLECT!
FOR DAYS! AND MONTHS! AND YEARS!
MAKING NEW THINGS! SO YOU CAN FIGHT STRONGER AND STRONGER MONSTERS!
TOILING AWAY UNTIL YOU CAN CRAFT THE ULTIMATE WEAPON!

I'LL SHOW YOU HOW IT'S DONE! BEHOLD! *THE CURSED BOOK OF ZOMBIE MAGIC!*

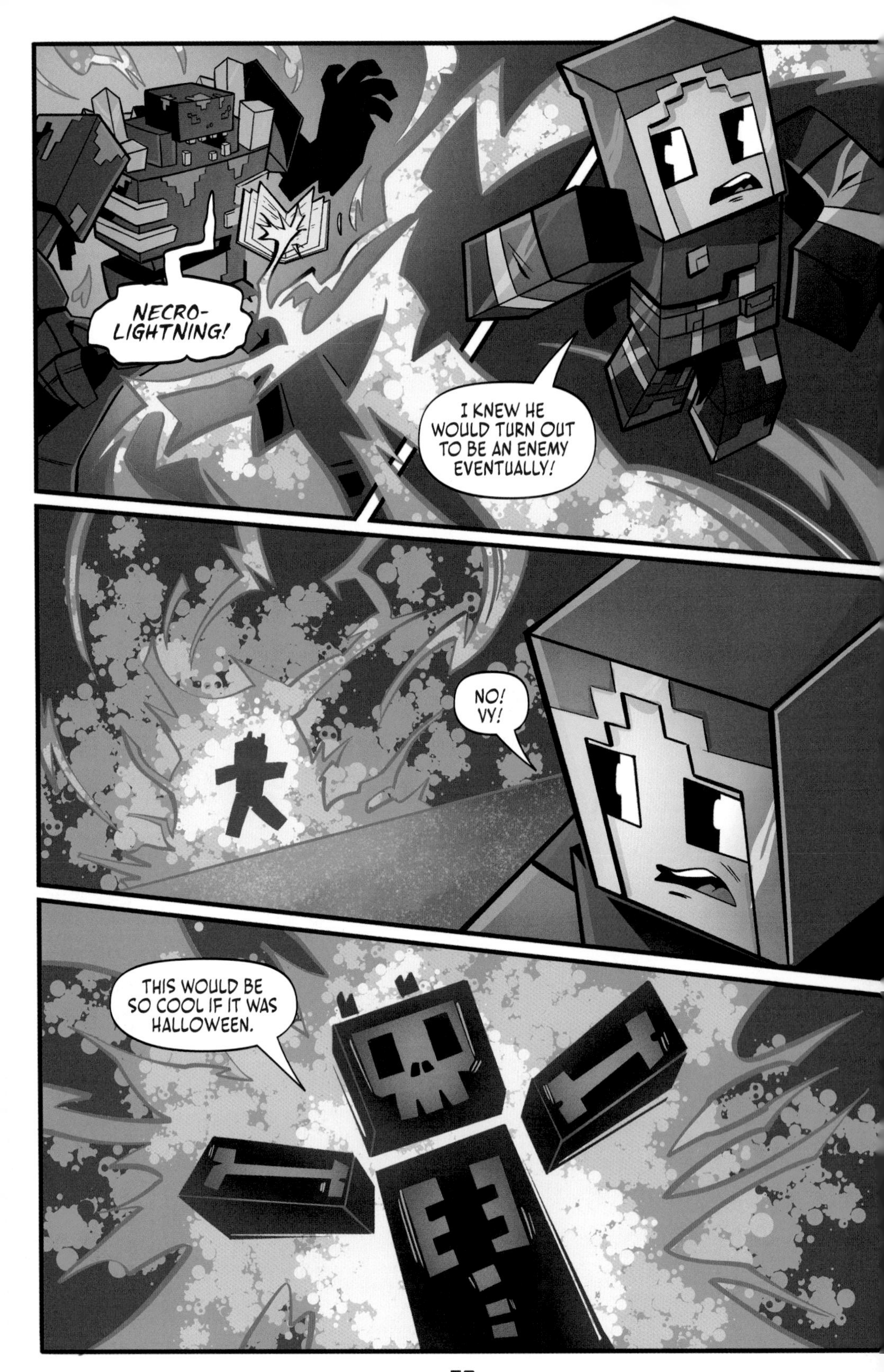
NECRO-LIGHTNING!
I KNEW HE WOULD TURN OUT TO BE AN ENEMY EVENTUALLY!
NO! VY!
THIS WOULD BE SO COOL IF IT WAS HALLOWEEN.

YOU WANT ME TO PLAY BY VIDEO GAME RULES? HERE WE GO!
SUPER-ULTRA-MAGIC . . . WHATEVER ATTACK I CAN DO WITH THIS STAFF!
POOT
WELL, THAT'S EMBARRASSING.
MAYBE YOU SHOULD HAVE SPENT MORE TIME CRAFTING A BETTER STAFF!

I WILL NEVER TAKE INTERNAL ORGANS FOR GRANTED AGAIN.
I PROMISE YOU, I WILL NEVER EAT ANOTHER HOT CHEETOS BURRITO . . . TWO NIGHTS IN A ROW.
MISSED US!

I WASN'T AIMING FOR YOU TWO . . . THIS TIME.

BEHOLD! THESE ARE ALL THE MIGHTY WARRIORS WHO NEVER BEAT THE TEMPLE.
WHAT MAKES YOU THINK YOU HAVE A CHANCE AGAINST ME AND THIS ARMY OF TRUE CRAFTERS?
BECAUSE WE KNOW HOW TO PLAY SMARTER, NOT HARDER. CHAD, CAST YOUR SPELL AGAIN AT THE ROOTS!
MAGIC TINY FIREBALL ATTACK!
SUPER-COOL ARMOR FLAME FAN!

FIRE!
BAD!
KEEP AWAY!
IMPOSSIBLE!
I DIDN'T THINK THAT'D WORK AT ALL.
NOOOOO!!!

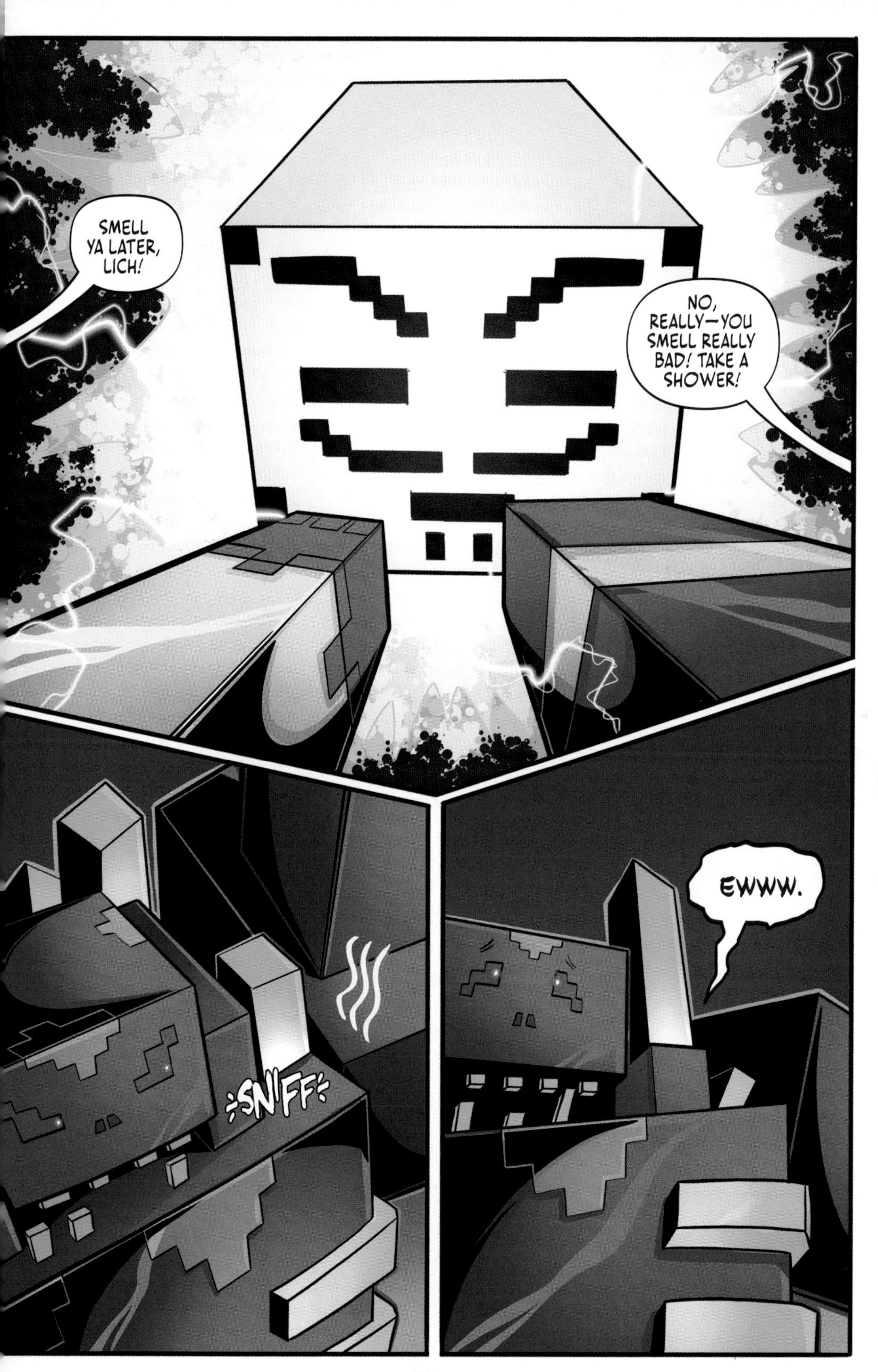
SMELL YA LATER, LICH!
NO, REALLY—YOU SMELL REALLY BAD! TAKE A SHOWER!
SNIFF
EWWW.

SO YOU REMEMBER THAT TIME I WAS ON THE ROOF AND MY LADDER FELL DOWN? WHILE YOU WERE WATCHING EVERY SUPERHERO MOVIE EVER MADE, I WAS STUCK ON THE ROOF FOR THREE DAYS.
THUMP THUMP THUMP
WE'VE TOLD YOU A THOUSAND TIMES, DANIEL, WE COULDN'T HEAR YOU YELLING OVER THE SOUNDS OF MOLE MAN FIGHTS AND BAD POP SOUNDTRACKS!
I'M STILL MAD . . . BUT WHILE I WAS UP THERE I TOOK THE OPPORTUNITY TO INSTALL MY LATEST GADGET.

SPY NINJAS
SAFE HOUSE
"BEHOLD! MY TINY AIR FORCE! MY MINIATURE SKY SOLDIERS!
"THE GIZMO DRONES!"

WAIT . . . WHY DO THEY ALL HAVE YOUR FACE ON THEM?
WELL . . . YOU KNOW . . .
THAT'S NOT IMPORTANT RIGHT NOW.
"WHAT'S IMPORTANT IS KEEPING THESE PROJECT ZORGO HACKERS BUSY!"
HEADQUARTERS! WE NEED BACKUP!

CHAPTER 4

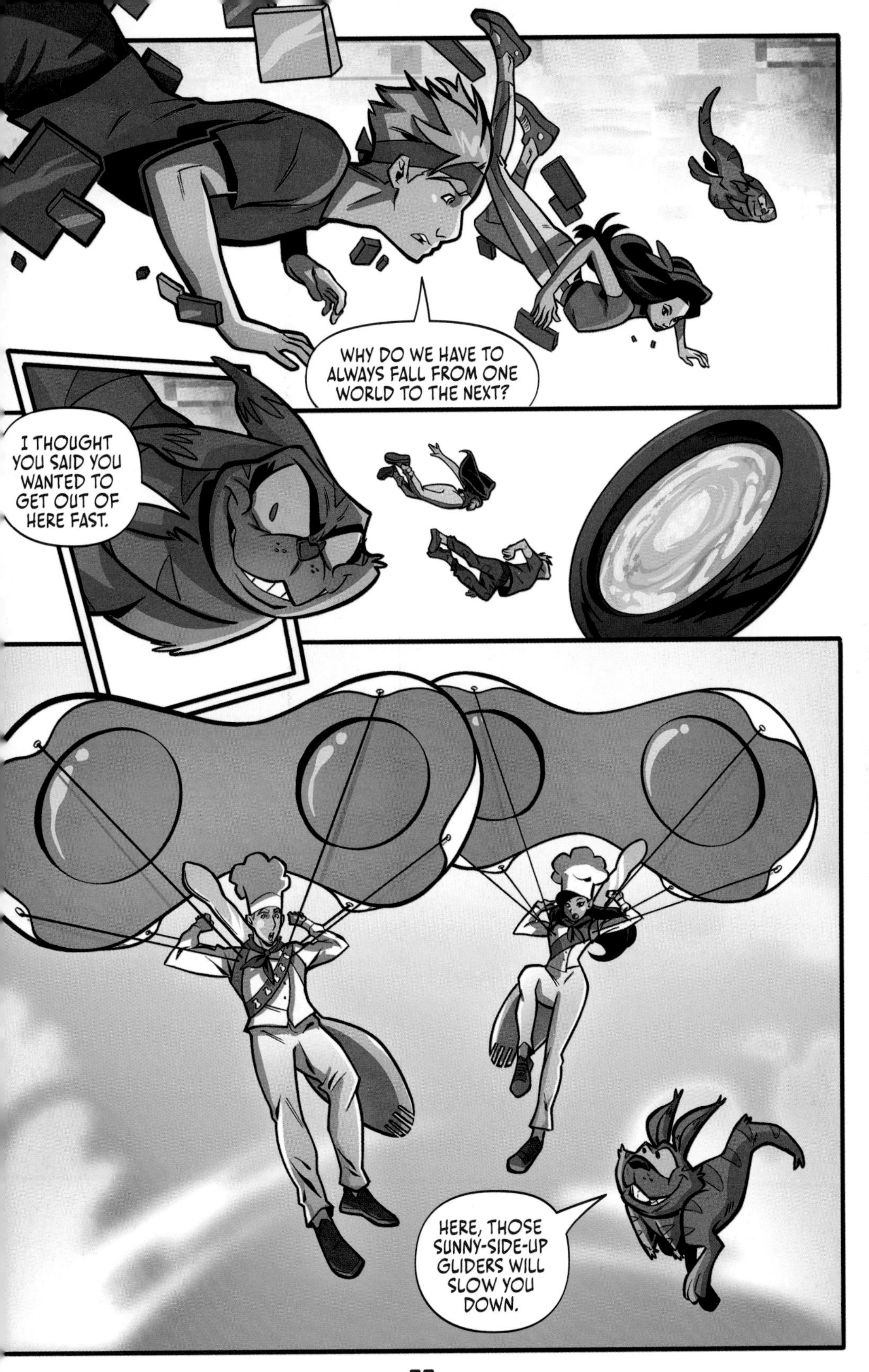
WHY DO WE HAVE TO ALWAYS FALL FROM ONE WORLD TO THE NEXT?
I THOUGHT YOU SAID YOU WANTED TO GET OUT OF HERE FAST.
HERE, THOSE SUNNY-SIDE-UP GLIDERS WILL SLOW YOU DOWN.

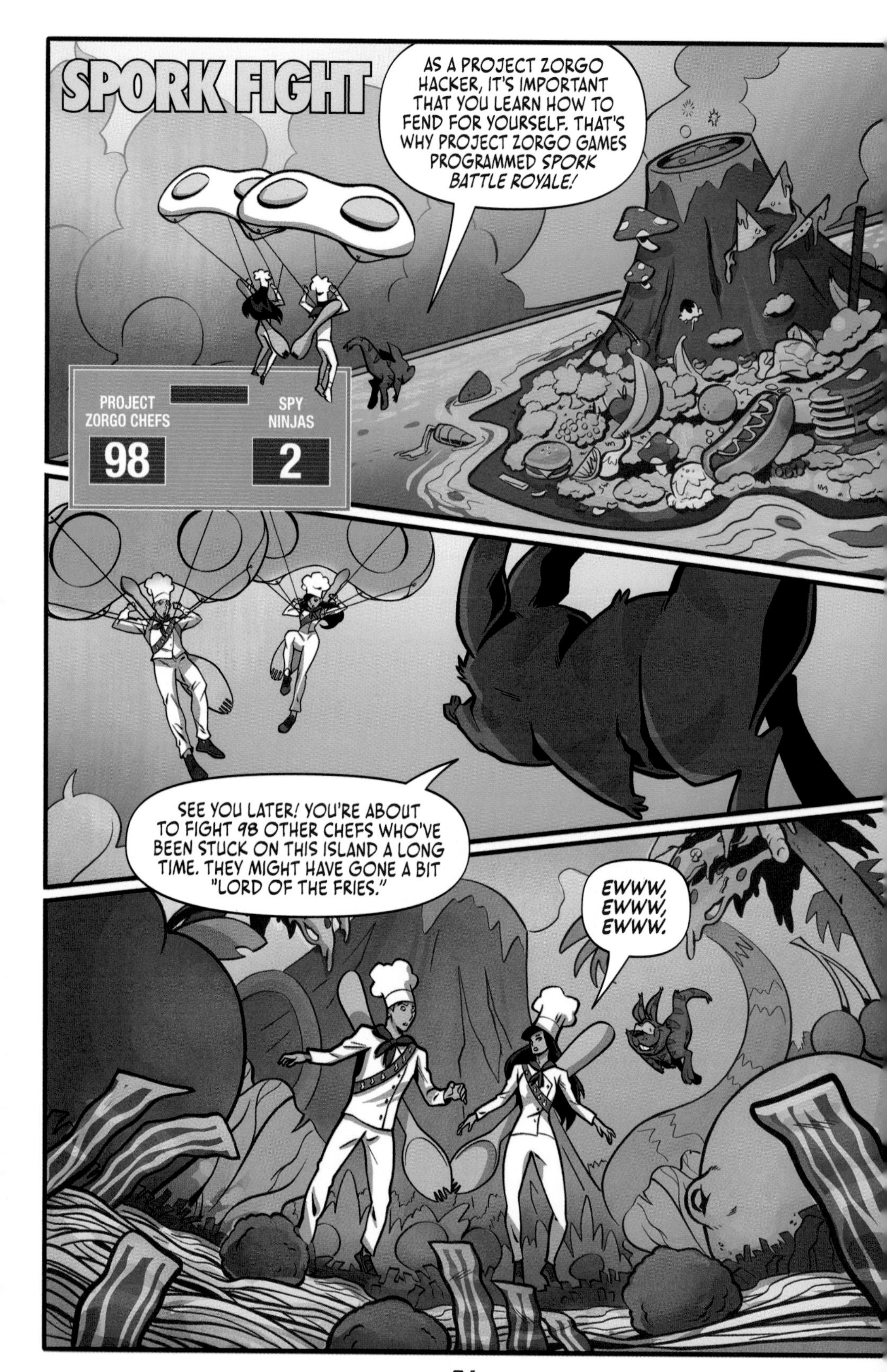
SPORK FIGHT
AS A PROJECT ZORGO HACKER, IT'S IMPORTANT THAT YOU LEARN HOW TO FEND FOR YOURSELF. THAT'S WHY PROJECT ZORGO GAMES PROGRAMMED SPORK BATTLE ROYALE!
PROJECT ZORGO CHEFS
98
SPY NINJAS
2
SEE YOU LATER! YOU'RE ABOUT TO FIGHT 98 OTHER CHEFS WHO'VE BEEN STUCK ON THIS ISLAND A LONG TIME. THEY MIGHT HAVE GONE A BIT "LORD OF THE FRIES."
EWWW, EWWW, EWWW.

SLY SAID THAT THERE WERE 98 ENEMIES ON THIS ISLAND.
WE'VE BEEN IN WORSE SPOTS BEFORE. WE JUST HAVE TO KEEP OUR COOL.
RUSTLE
RUSTLE
OH, IT'S JUST A LITTLE ICE CREAM CONE-ARY . . .

AND A WHOLE SWARM OF ENEMY CHEFS!

AHH! THIS IS WHY I DON'T LIKE HOT SAUCE!
WHY MUST DELICIOUS SPICE HURT SO BAD?
NO WAY WE CAN TAKE ON THAT MANY ENEMIES AT ONE TIME.
CAN WE PLAY IT A BIT SAFER NOW? I'M ON MY LAST LIFE.
OKAY, OKAY.

WAIT. WHAT IS THAT DELICIOUS SMELL?

I DON'T KNOW. EVERYTHING SMELLS SURPRISINGLY GOOD AROUND HERE, EVEN IF IT'S GROSS THAT IT'S ALL JUST SITTING OUTSIDE.

NO, LIKE REALLY DELICIOUS. LIKE THE TASTE OF SOME-THING WARM ON A RAINY DAY.
WAIT! I THOUGHT WE WERE BEING MORE CAREFUL!

C'MON, QUICKLY!
SORRY IF I'M STILL A LITTLE SCARED OF LAVA AFTER THE FIRST LEVEL.
THIS VOLCANO ISN'T FILLED WITH BUBBLING LAVA!
IT'S . . .
IT'S BUBBLING BROTH!
I'VE GOT AN IDEA THAT WILL TAKE OUT ALL THE OTHER CHEFS IN ONE FELL SWOOP.

YOU JUST HAVE TO FOLLOW MY RECIPE AND AVOID OTHER PLAYERS.
"TO HELP SEASON THE BROTH, WE'LL NEED A FEW OTHER INGREDIENTS.
"ONIONS.
"RICE NOODLES.
"GINGER.
"FISH SAUCE.
"A FEW OTHER TASTY SPICES!"
AND SECRET INGREDIENTS FOR THE BROTH THAT I'LL NEVER TELL ANYONE. NOT EVEN CHAD.
SALT
CLOVES
CARDAMOM

"AND YOU CAN'T HAVE THIS RECIPE WITHOUT TOPPINGS.
"HERBS.
"PEPPERS.
"BEAN SPROUTS.
"LIMES.
"AND DON'T FORGET THE HOISIN AND SRIRACHA SAUCE!"

NOW WE HAVE A DELICIOUS GIANT PHO THAT NO ONE COULD RESIST.
THEY'RE ALREADY ON THEIR WAY!
AHHH, I HAVEN'T EVEN HAD ANY.

WHAT IS THAT DELICIOUS SMELL?
I HAVEN'T EATEN ANYTHING THAT WASN'T SITTING ON THE GROUND IN SO LONG.
HERE'S ANOTHER RECIPE!

MENTOS
DIET SODA
TAKE LOTS OF MENTOS AND DIET SODA . . .
MIX THEM TOGETHER.
PROJECT ZORGO CHEFS
SPY NINJAS
0
2
SPY NINJAS WIN!
"AND YOU GET QUITE THE CHEMICAL REACTION!"

EWWW, CHAD.
WHAT? IT'S STILL GOOD. JUST A LITTLE SWEETER.
I DON'T KNOW HOW YOU DID IT, BUT YOU DID.
THE NEXT WORLD IS ONLY GOING TO GET HARDER, THOUGH, MATES.

MAN, THESE HACKERS ARE SO LAME!
WE'VE GOT THEM BEAT!
EVEN WITHOUT A PLUNGE-CHUCK.

I'M SURE THEY THINK THEY HAVE US BEAT. BUT NOW THEY'LL HAVE TO CONTEND WITH . . .
PROJECT ZORGOMONGOUS!

WHERE SPY NINJAS?! ME HATE SPY NINJAS! ME PUNCH SPY NINJAS!

THIS IS NO PROBLEM, I'M SURE THE DRONES CAN HANDLE IT.
I'M NOT SO SURE.

PUNY LITTLE FLIES NOT SPY NINJAS!
BRING ME REAL FIGHTERS!
Psst.
WHO THERE?!

MASTER OF DISGUISE KICK!
PLUNGECHUCK-LESS PUMMEL!
GIZMETEOR HAMMER!

THAT TICKLED.
NOW ME FIGHT FOR REAL!

CHAPTER 5

101101110011010100110000101110011011100
000101110011011100110111000011
1110000011110010
100110
0101
01

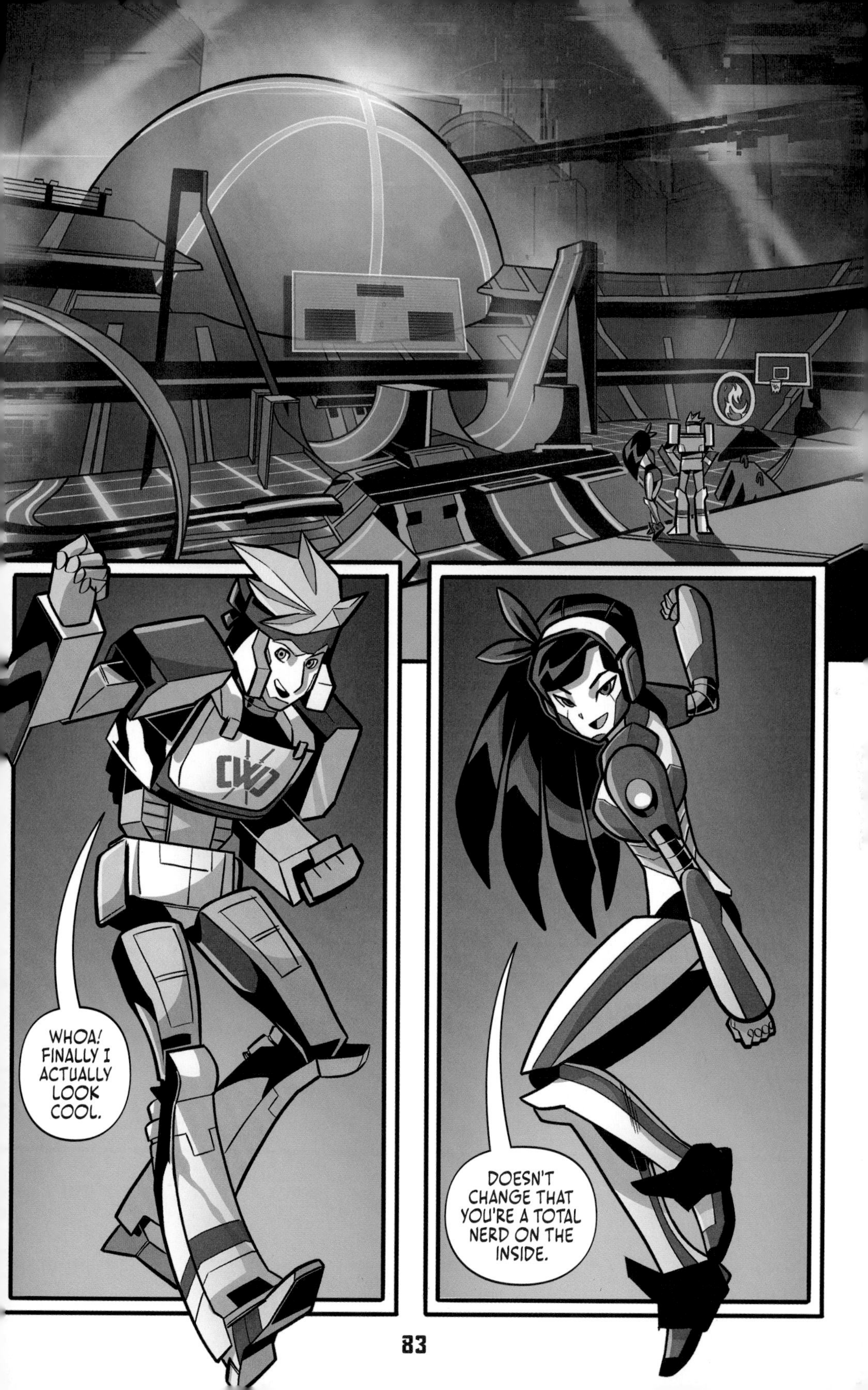
WHOA! FINALLY I ACTUALLY LOOK COOL.
DOESN'T CHANGE THAT YOU'RE A TOTAL NERD ON THE INSIDE.

TRY TRANSFORMING, CHAD. SEE WHAT YOU LOOK LIKE IN YOUR VEHICLE FORM.
BEEP BEEP
OH, YOU'RE SO CUTE!
WELL, WHAT DO YOU TRANSFORM INTO?
HONK HONK
URRRRROOOOOOM

YOU'VE GOT TO BE KIDDING ME.
ARE THESE REALLY THE FIRST CHUMPS TO MAKE IT TO OUR LEVEL, CIRCUIT BREAKER?
TO THINK THAT WE'VE BEEN WAITING ALL THIS TIME FOR THESE TWO SCRAP HEAPS.
I ASSUME YOU'RE THE OPPOSING TEAM.

NOW, NOW, TIRE FIRE, I'M SURE THEY WILL BE WORTHY OPPONENTS.
TRULY, I HAVE WAITED FOR ETERNITÀ TO MEET SUCH A MACCHINA BELLA.

GETTING A LITTLE
HOT UNDER THE COLLAR,
PLAYER 1?

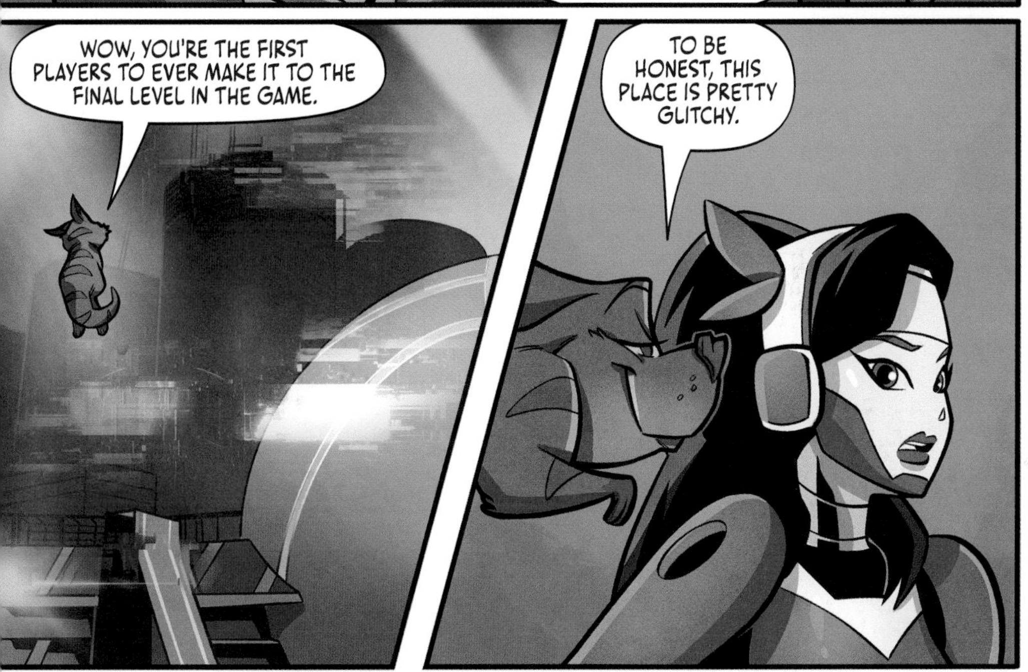
WOW, YOU'RE THE FIRST
PLAYERS TO EVER MAKE IT TO THE
FINAL LEVEL IN THE GAME.
TO BE
HONEST, THIS
PLACE IS PRETTY
GLITCHY.

WELCOME TO
THE WORLD OF
RACER BRAWL!
PROJECT
ZORGOBOTS
0
SPY
NINJAS
0

PART BASKETBALL, PART FORMULA 1 RACING, RACER BRAWL WILL TEST YOUR ABILITY TO FOLLOW THE RULES AND THINK FAST.

DON'T PLAN ON GETTING OUT WITH ONLY SCRATCHED PAINT.
NEVER AWARDED BEFORE, THE WINNERS GET THE COVETED PROJECT ZORGO CHAMPIONSHIP TROPHY!
I WANT TO SMASH IT UP IN MY COMPACTOR.
NOT SO FAST, BUDDY—THAT'S OUR TICKET OUT OF HERE.
I HOPE NEITHER OF US WINS, BELLA, SO WE CAN SPEND MORE TIME TOGETHER.
YOU'VE OFFICIALLY GONE FROM CHARMING TO CREEPY.

LET'S PLAY SOME RACER BRAWL!
THEY CAN'T GET THE BALL IF IT'S INSIDE MY LITTLE CABIN.

YIKES!
BZZZZTTTT
OUCH.
TRAVEL! BALL GOES TO PROJECT ZORGOBOTS!
THIS IS GOING TO BE TOO EASY.
I COME ALL THIS WAY, AND THE GAME'S GONNA BE OVER IN A COUPLE MINUTES.

MAKE IT PAINLESS, AMICO.
DON'T WORRY, I WON'T.
FWEEET!
FIRST TECHNICAL FOUL ON WILD CLAY.
BUT HE HIT ME?!
HE WAS IN PEDESTRIAN FORM. YOUR FAULT FOR HITTING HIM AS A CAR.

ALL RIGHT, GARBAGE TRUCK! HAND IT OVER.
FAT CHANCE, PIPSQUEAK.

CIAO. SO GOOD TO SEE YOU AGAIN, MIO AMORE.

ARRIVEDERCI, I CAN'T SAY THE SAME.
FWEEET!
FOUL BY QWAINT ON CIRCUIT BREAKER.

C'MON, REF! YOU CAN'T BE SERIOUS! THAT GUY'S A CREEP.
FWEEET!
SECOND TECHNICAL FOUL BY WILD CLAY FOR APPROACHING THE REF IN A THREATENING MANNER.

YOU'RE *OUT* OF THE GAME, PUNK!
ZAAAAPP
UGH!
OOF! ROUGH GAME, PLAYER 1.

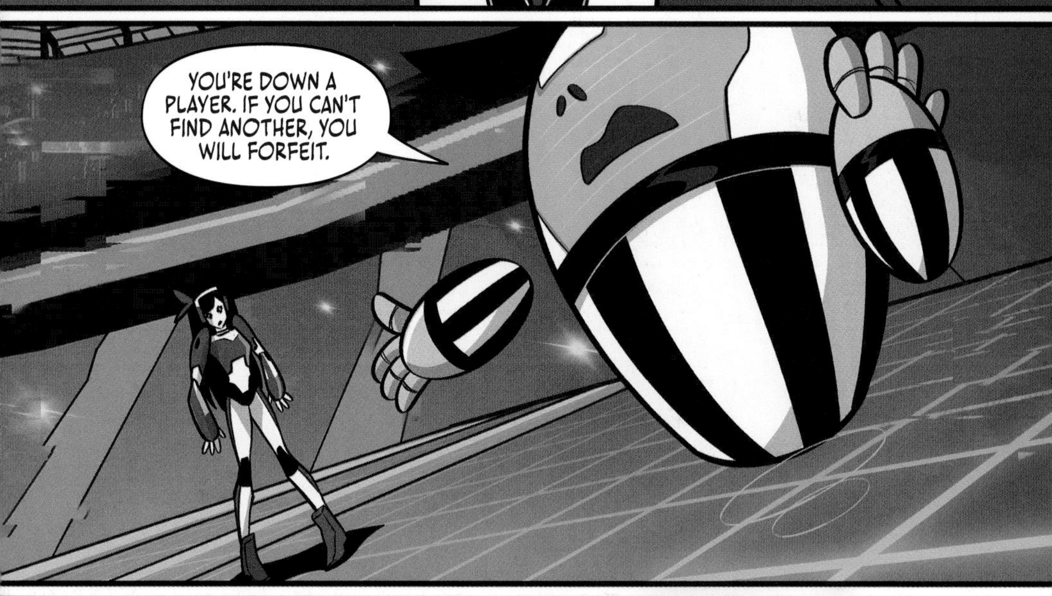
YOU'RE DOWN A PLAYER. IF YOU CAN'T FIND ANOTHER, YOU WILL FORFEIT.

SORRY, VY!

DON'T WORRY. I HAVE ONE.

YOU DO?

OUR SUBSTITUTION IS . . . SLY MARSUPIAL.

WHO? LITTLE OL' ME?
I GUESS EVERY ADORABLE MASCOT IS CURSED TO DO A SPORTS CROSSOVER.
HOLD UP, BUDDY!
THIS HAS TO BE AGAINST THE RULES. YOU KNOW WHO SHE IS RIGHT? THAT'S—
SPY NINJAS

SPY SAM—BZZZTTT—SLY MARSUPIAL HAS JOINED THE SPY NINJAS!
BEEN A WHILE SINCE I HAD THE CHANCE TO SHOW OFF MY OWN SICK STUNTS.
JUST A WARM-UP FOR WHAT'S AHEAD, I GUESS.

SPY NINJAS
∞
PROJECT ZORGOBOTS
0

THEY HAD NO CHANCE AGAINST A BOSS LIKE ME!
THEY SURE DIDN'T.

ARE YOU TWO READY TO GO HOME?

HOW DO YOU THINK THE REST OF THE SPY NINJAS ARE DOING?

"I'M SURE THEY'RE DOING JUST FINE."
CRASH
WAY TO GO, BIG GUY!

LUCKY FOR US THE BIG GUY ISN'T AS SMART AS HE IS STRONG.
LET'S SEE HOW "NOT SMART" HE IS.
GRRR! SPY NINJAS!
ME SMASH! SPY NINJAS!

THAT SHOULD BUY US SOME TIME TO GET TO THE MOST SECURE ROOM IN THE WHOLE HOUSE.

CRASH
BAM
SMASH
WHO KNEW WE HAD SO MANY COATRACKS?

ME FIND YOU SPY NINJAS AND ME *SMASH!*

SLAM
WAIT A MINUTE?! OUR LAST STAND'S GOING TO BE IN . . .

THE BATHROOM?!

CHAPTER 6

WAIT, WASN'T THAT SUPPOSED TO BE THE LAST LEVEL?
THAT'S WHAT SLY SAID . . .
IT'S BEAUTIFUL, BUT IT'S JUST BITS AND PIECES.

THERE'S SLY! IS THIS THE END?
OH, IT CERTAINLY IS, CHAD. YOU BEAT THE FINAL LEVEL.
WAIT. . . SHE KNOWS MY NAME?

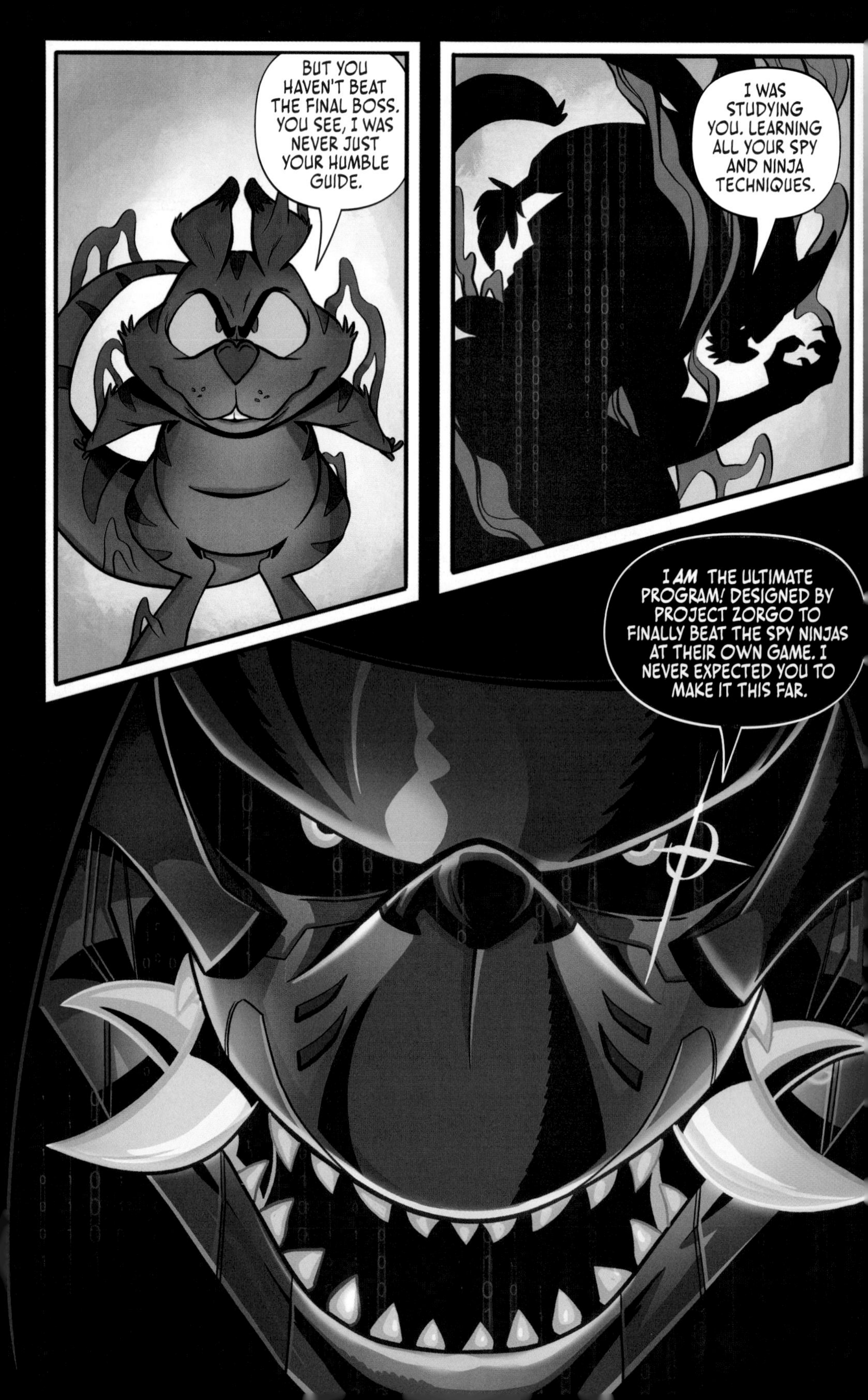
BUT YOU HAVEN'T BEAT THE FINAL BOSS. YOU SEE, I WAS NEVER JUST YOUR HUMBLE GUIDE.
I WAS STUDYING YOU. LEARNING ALL YOUR SPY AND NINJA TECHNIQUES.
I *AM* THE ULTIMATE PROGRAM! DESIGNED BY PROJECT ZORGO TO FINALLY BEAT THE SPY NINJAS AT THEIR OWN GAME. I NEVER EXPECTED YOU TO MAKE IT THIS FAR.

I AM SPY SAMURAI X!!
IT WILL BE EASY TO TAKE YOUR LAST LIVES!

YAAAHHHH!!!
SHWING
YOU KNOW I NEVER LIKED THIS KANGAROO.
ME EITHER.

KRACKABOOM
WE CAN'T STAY ON THE DEFENSE.
LOOK! OVER THERE!
A LOOT CRATE!

YOU GO FOR IT. I'LL DISTRACT HER. I'M A SMALLER TARGET, AFTER ALL.
HEY, YOU BIG KANGAROO! I'M "DOWN UNDER" HERE!
G'DAY, MATE . . .

WELL, THIS IS CERTAINLY AN UPGRADE.
C'MON, SLY! CAN'T WE GO BACK TO THE FUN TIMES LIKE LEVEL 1?
THE FUN TIMES?! *THE FUN TIMES?!*
FOR MY ENTIRE EXISTENCE, I'VE EITHER BEEN TRAINING PROJECT ZORGO HACKERS OR SITTING IN MY CONTROL ROOM.

WAITING FOR THE DAY I'D GET TO USE MY SKILLS AGAINST YOU.
HEY, SLY!
TRY PICKING ON SOMEONE WITH THE SAME STAT BOOSTS.

SLY! YOU DON'T HAVE TO DO THIS! WE DON'T HAVE TO FIGHT. YOU CAN JUST LET US GO.
IT'S IN MY PROGRAMMING! I HAVE TO DELETE YOU SPY NINJAS!
WHILE THEY'RE HAVING THEIR EMOTIONAL SAMURAI SHOWDOWN, I'LL TRY TO FIND THAT CONTROL ROOM SHE TALKED ABOUT.
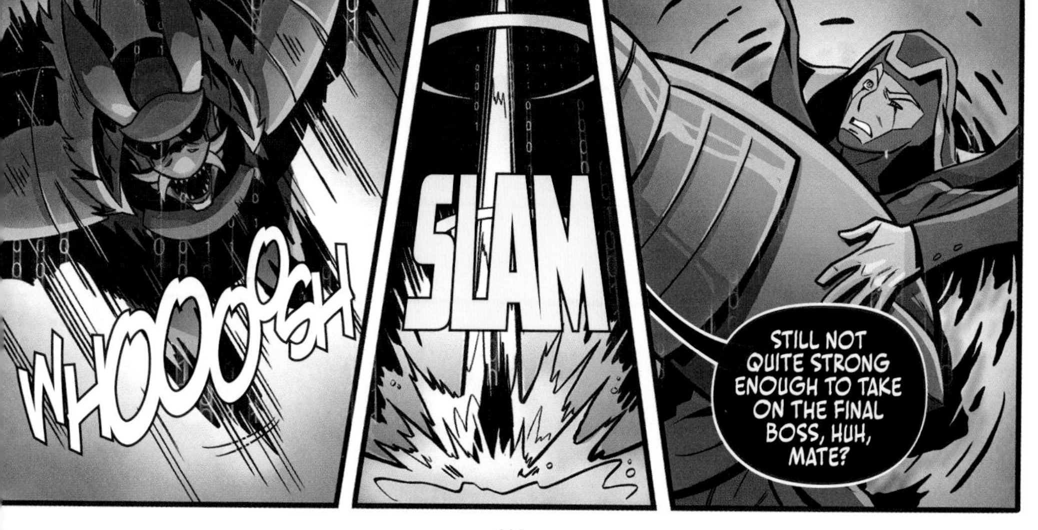
WHOOOOSH
SLAM
STILL NOT QUITE STRONG ENOUGH TO TAKE ON THE FINAL BOSS, HUH, MATE?

WAIT, WHAT'S THAT TINY GLITCH?
VY! I'LL HOLD OFF SLY!

YOU INVESTIGATE WHATEVER'S BEHIND THAT WEIRD SMALL DOOR!
I'LL BE BACK, CHAD!

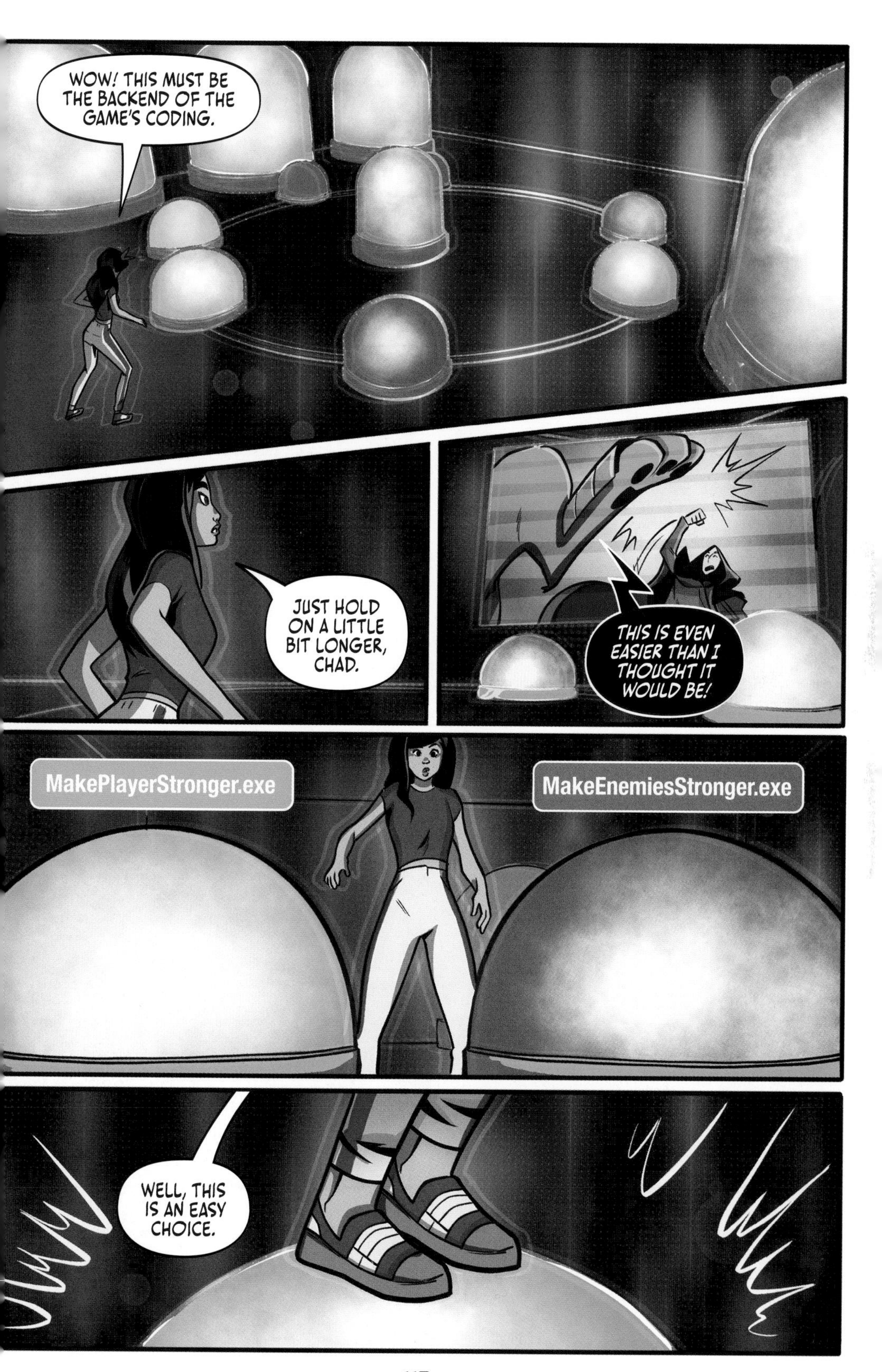
WOW! THIS MUST BE THE BACKEND OF THE GAME'S CODING.
JUST HOLD ON A LITTLE BIT LONGER, CHAD.
THIS IS EVEN EASIER THAN I THOUGHT IT WOULD BE!
MakePlayerStronger.exe
MakeEnemiesStronger.exe
WELL, THIS IS AN EASY CHOICE.

POWER UP
WHAT?! HOW ARE YOU THIS STRONG?
SUPER FLAME ATTACK—MAXED STATS!
OH, HELLO!
BrainWashReset.exe
THE CONTROL ROOM! SHE FOUND ALL THE CHEAT CODES!

WAIT . . . WHERE ARE WE?
LAST I REMEMBER I PUT A VR HEADSET ON.
OH NO! I LEFT A BURRITO IN THE MICROWAVE! IT'S GOING TO BE COLD NOW.
THIS ISN'T POSSIBLE! YOU'RE BREAKING ALL THE RULES!
THAT'S THE KANGAROO!
SHE'S THE ONE WHO KEPT US HERE.
LIGHTNING . . . PLAYERS! I'VE GOT AN IDEA!

RAISE UP HER SWORD.
LIGHTNING IS ATTRACTED TO HIGH, POINTY OBJECTS!
KRACKA BOOOM
OUCH!
HP 0%
I WAS JUST... PLAYING... THE GAME...

WHO WOULD HAVE THOUGHT PROJECT ZORGO WOULD LABEL EVERYTHING SO CLEARLY?
SendEveryoneHome.exe

THAT WAS AWESOME!
WE SHOULD PLAY AGAIN SOMETIME.
MAYBE A DIFFERENT GAME, THOUGH.

FINALLY! I CAN EAT THAT COLD BURRITO!

YOU DONE GAMING FOR THE DAY?
I THINK I'VE HAD ENOUGH SCREEN TIME.

I ALWAYS KNEW IT WOULD GO DOWN THIS WAY.
SMASH
SMASH

JUST LIKE ELVIS . . .
I WOULD DIE IN THE BATHROOM.
YIKES.
UGH . . . MY HEAD . . .
THIS IS NOT WHAT I EXPECTED TO WAKE UP TO.

STATUS UPDATE?

PROJECT ZORGO TRACED US.
AND DROPPED A SUPER HACKER ON OUR HOUSE.
AND WE LOCKED OURSELVES IN THE BATHROOM.

OKAY, WE WERE HOPING THINGS WOULD BE GOING A BIT BETTER IRL . . .
BUT THIS IS A BIT WORSE . . .

MELVIN, WHY AM I SITTING ON YOUR WEIRD PROJECT ZORGO PLUNGER?

THE PLUNGECHUCK!
MELVIN! THE DOOR!

CRASH
MUCH LIKE DANIEL, I KNEW THIS DAY WOULD COME . . .
. . . WHEN I WOULD USE THE PLUNGECHUCK IN BATTLE.
BUTTERFLY KICK!

ME FELT THAT!
THERE'S MORE WHERE THAT CAME FROM.
GRRRRR!!!
NOT SO FAST!

MAYBE SOME SCREEN TIME WILL HELP YOU CHILL OUT.
WAIT . . . DID TH PLUNGECHUCK ACTUALLY SAVE THE DAY?

I THOUGHT THAT PROJECT WAS ABANDONED AS A FAILURE?
SO. . .WHAT DO WE DO ABOUT THE BIG GUY?
I'LL CALL UP PROJECT ZORGO HEADQUARTERS WITH THE TRACKING DEVICE AND SEE WHEN THEY WANT TO PICK HIM UP FROM HIS PLAYDATE.
THIS IS THE LAST GAMER I'M DRAGGING AROUND THE HOUSE TODAY.
I WONDER WHAT THE BIG GUY IS SEEING RIGHT NOW . . .
ME IN VIDEO GAME?
SNIFF
SNIFF

THERE, THERE SAD LITTLE ROOROO. WHAT WRONG?
ALL MY FRIENDS LEFT BECAUSE I COULDN'T HELP BUT BE MEAN.
ME BEEN MEAN TODAY, TOO. ME WANT TO TRY JUST BEING NICE NOW.
HOW DO YOU FEEL ABOUT BASKETBALL?
ME LIKE TO DUNK.
SO WHO WANTS TO PLAY VIDEO GAMES?
I'D RATHER CLEAN ALL THE BATHROOMS.
THAT'S EXACTLY WHAT YOU PROMISED ME!
YOU CAN USE THE PLUNGECHUCK!
MISSION: Complete

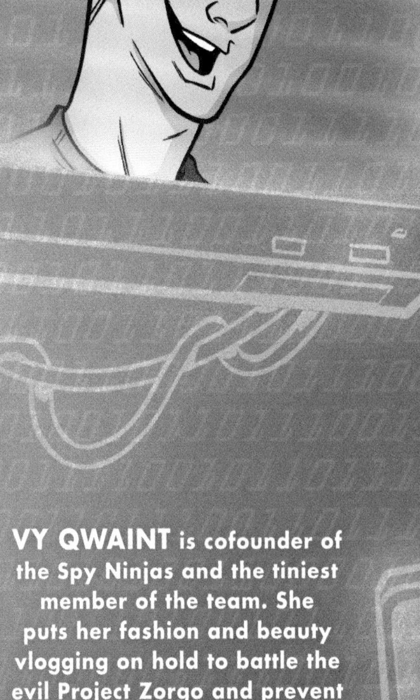

CHAD WILD CLAY is a YouTuber who learned martial arts at a young age and developed an affinity for slicing fruits with ninja gadgets. After a hacker illegally deleted a handful of his videos, Chad and Vy Qwaint formed the Spy Ninjas in order to stop the evil Project Zorgo from hacking the rest of YouTube. Using his height, speed, and strength, he can fight his way out of any situation, especially when he has his stun-chucks in hand. Although his impressive martial arts and ninja skills make him an incredible fighter, he lives his life promoting kindness, self-defense, and lighthearted humor.

VY

VY QWAINT is cofounder of the Spy Ninjas and the tiniest member of the team. She puts her fashion and beauty vlogging on hold to battle the evil Project Zorgo and prevent them from ruining the internet. Also known as the "Spicy Spy Ninja," she is always prepared to go head-to-head with evil hackers, using her stealth, spy skills, and small size to outwit them. On the surface, Vy is petite, giggly, and silly, but don't let that fool you! Her ability to throw kicks, solve difficult puzzles, and pick even the hardest of locks make her a force to be reckoned with.

VANNOTES

VANNOTES is a writer, cartoonist, and educator based out of Idaho. Their previous work includes *Bendy: Crack-Up Comics Collection* with publications from Scholastic, King Features Syndicate, and Boom! Studios. They received their Bachelor of Fine Arts in Comic Art from the Minneapolis College of Art and Design and their Master of Fine Arts in Creative Writing from Eastern Oregon University. They were named Treasure Valley Community College's Student Advocate of the Year in 2021. In their free time, they read way too many comics and play far too many video games.

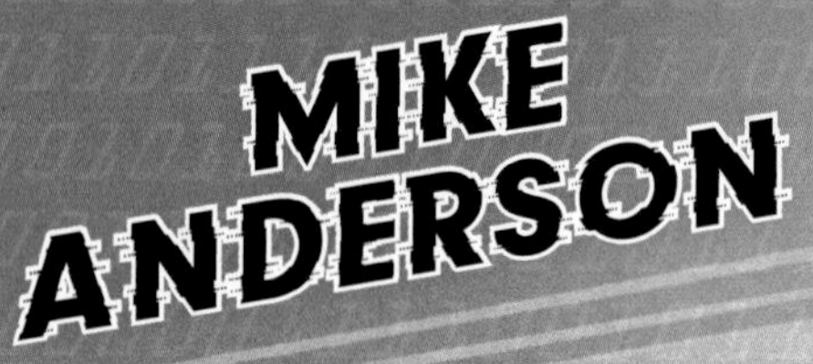

MIKE ANDERSON

MIKE is a comic book artist from Oklahoma, where he lives with his wife, Heather, and three sons Colt, Koda, and Caden. Mike has done work for several indie and mainstream comic publishers, as well as illustration and animation work for many national brands. Born and raised on the '80s and '90s craze of Ninja Turtles, Mike was all too excited to work on the Spy Ninjas graphic novel. When he is not drawing comics, Mike enjoys playing with his kids, animating, and scarfing lots of pizza! You can find more of his work at MikeyComix.com.